THE REWARD FROM ABOVE

To Grandma Nola

[signature]

Josh Melton

PUBLISH AMERICA

PublishAmerica
Baltimore

ISBN: 978-1-4489-8806-8
PUBLISHED BY PUBLISHAMERICA, LLLP
www.publishamerica.com
Baltimore

Printed in the United States of America

Preface

I've always wanted to leave this world with a life that I could be proud of, that anyone would be proud of. I wanted my life to have a meaning. Being forgotten was not an option that I would be satisfied with. I just wish I would have had more time.

I can't complain though. I would get my wish. People would be proud of me. When they spoke my name they would think "Hero." Parents would want their kids to grow up to be as selfless as me. They would forget about the first twenty-eight years of my life. All they would remember is how it ended.

Dying for the greater good. Who would have expected that out of me? I wouldn't have before today. I was a nobody. I have accomplished nothing. I have helped no one. It's never even crossed my mind.

If I would have just ignored my instincts for those few seconds I would still be alive. All it would have taken was for me to look away; turn my back and head in the other direction. But who would remember me? What would my life had meant when I finally left this world? Nothing.

So if you're asking me if giving my life for this was worth it. Yes. Yes it was.

Chapter 1
Another Day

I woke to the same monotonous tone of the alarm clock that had been waking me up for the last ten years. It was a chilly twenty-three degrees in Knoxville, tiny flakes of snow were fluttering down from the pale gray sky. I was wearing the same work clothes that I'd been wearing all week; black Dickie pants and a gray button up work shirt with a white name plate on the left breast that read Jaycin. I had many pairs of the black pants and the gray shirts but why dirty up more when the ones I had been wearing all week were still bearable to smell.

Lying in the center of downtown Knoxville is a small factory that manufactures air bags to go into cars. I have been working at this factory since the day I graduated high school. I hate it. My dad is my boss and I hate that also. Not that he's a bad guy, because he's not. He's actually a pretty great guy. I just hate that all my co-workers seem to hold it against me. They think that I get special treatment, and maybe I do, but how is that my fault? Some of the people have been there over thirty years. I've been there ten and I was just promoted to be my dad's second man. That has a lot of those guys in a pretty foul mood.

It doesn't really matter to me what they think about me; I hate everyone that works there with the exception of my dad. I hate having to do the same thing over and over day after day. I mean making air bags. Come on. How many different ways is there to make an air bag. When I'm at work all I can think about is how I'm wasting my life here. I'll never get the last ten years of my life back, they're gone forever.

On the other hand I did love Knoxville. There is a lot of stuff for a young guy like me to get into around here. Bars with lots of amazing looking college girls that like to drink and forget about their morals, and sports to watch year round. What else could a single guy want?

My Phone was ringing.

"Hey son! You ready for work?" My dad called out from the other end of the phone.

"Yea I'm ready."

"Well I'll be over to pick you up in about ten minutes."

Every since my dad promoted me, we work the same hours and he insists that we ride to work together. I live in a pretty nice apartment in downtown Knoxville, so it wouldn't take me five minutes to walk to work, but still yet he thinks it gives us some time to talk about my role in the company and how and what I could do to improve. I wasn't really in the mood for this today. Any day really, but especially today.

"You know what dad, I would really rather walk today."

"Are you crazy? It's freezing outside."

"I'll wear a coat. It's no big deal. I've got some things on my mind and I think walking to work today could really do me some good."

"Ok then. I'll see you in a bit. Be careful."

"I will. Bye dad."

I grabbed my coat from the hall way closet and walked out my door and into the elevator.

As I walked out of the door, I was hit not by the cold, but by the beauty of the city as the first snow of the winter fell to the ground. I could tell I wasn't the only one. Most all of the people were looking to the sky with a comforting smile on their faces. It took away some of the anguish I felt about having to spend another wasted day at the air bag factory.

There was a lot of street traffic this morning but mostly people walking and shopping. There weren't many cars traveling the road at all. It was early morning so there were lots of parents holding their children's hands on their way to school. Then there were some people, like me, who were enjoying a nice walk to work. The rest of the people were shoppers who wanted to get an early jump on Christmas shopping.

The kids on their way to school seemed to be getting the most enjoyment of this first snow. Every kid I looked at was laughing or catching snowflakes in their mouths or in their tiny hands. It was the most amazing thing to see how one small act of nature could light up the faces in these kids. It was as if they had never seen snow before and they never would again.

My spirits had been slightly lifted as I passed laughing kid after laughing kid and smiling adult after smiling adult. The only thing keeping this from being a perfect trip to work was the one small child who was screaming in horror as if his favorite cartoon character had just died of cancer.

The child had to be around three years old. He had on a massive jacket with a hood over his head so I would imagine he wasn't upset about being cold. His mother held his hand in hers but he didn't seem to be struggling to get away so that mustn't have been it either. The mother didn't even seem to notice his screams. She never once glanced down at the young boy. Looking around it seemed that no one was noticing this child's screams except for me. Even the people that passed the mother and child never once glanced in their direction.

Just as I was about to give up trying to figure out what was wrong with this kid and move on, he stopped screaming and looked directly at me. I stared back and our eyes were locked in a gaze. Never in my life had I seen such an intense look from such a young child. It was no longer like I was staring into a child's eyes, but something more. It was if the eyes were trying to tell me something that I couldn't comprehend.

I was frozen in my tracks. I physically couldn't move. Something was making me stay there and keep looking into those eyes. Suddenly the child's eyes moved away towards the middle of the street. It was only for a second, and then the eyes were right back into mine.

I had to break his gaze. I wanted to see what he had looked at. What could it have been that broke the intense stare that we had going? I looked to the middle of the street where the young child had just looked. There was nothing there except what looked to be a young kid, thirteen or fourteen years old wearing a school uniform, listening to an iPod and had a backpack thrown over his shoulder.

When I looked back at the young child he was still staring at me, only this time the child's eyes were wider and more frightened now than intense. He glanced back to the kid in the middle of the street, then back to me. It didn't seem like it could be possible but his eyes were even wider this time. I took another look at the kid in the street. He was just walking down the center of the road. He looked normal, just as any other kid on their way to school.

Over his shoulder I seen a black SUV turn the corner and start heading in this direction. It was still a good ways off but I yelled at the kid to move out of the road. He couldn't hear me. I yelled again but he still didn't move. His head never rose up from the focus he had at the lines in the center of the road.

Without noticing, I had been walking closer to the boy as I was yelling at him. The SUV was also getting closer. I was waiting for it to show some signs of slowing down, but there was none. I looked into the windshield of the oncoming car; it was a young mother and her young daughter in a car seat sitting next to her. It looked like she was trying to hand something to her daughter. She was paying no attention to the road.

I looked back at the young child across the street. His eyes were no longer looking at me. They were focused on the young kid in the street. I had no time left to think. I took off running to the center of the street. The woman in the SUV looked up and seen me and slammed on her brakes. They didn't work. The snow on the road had made it slick and she started sliding right at the kid. I could see the terror in her eyes as she knew what she was about to do. I tried running faster and it seemed to be working. I felt like I was running faster than I ever had in my life. The SUV was closing in. I leapt at the boy and knocked him towards the sidewalk. He was safely at a distance from the SUV. I was a lot closer, but the SUV came to stop just inches before running me over.

I was safe but my heart was pounding at a highly accelerated rate. Everyone that was nearby suddenly was making their way to the street. Some of them check to see if I'm ok. I was except for a sharp pain I was feeling in my head. There was no blood. I know because I heard some guy say, "Hey, there's no blood."

Most everyone else had moved on now to the startled young kid that I had knocked out of the way. He was fine too, but he was young so they were worried about him. The pain in my head was getting stronger. I started to get up but I was feeling dizzy so I lay back down. I closed my eyes for a second and when I opened them back up someone was standing over me. It was the child whose gaze led me to save the young kid.

"You just did a great thing."

"What? What are you, like three?"

"Four actually, but who's counting."

"How did you know what was happening? Why were you looking at me like that? Who is that kid? Who are you?"

"That's a lot of questions. Well, who I am is an angel. I was sent here to protect that kid. I knew what was going to happen because I seen it coming before hand. I was looking at you because I knew you were the only one down here that would have helped him. And he is Daniel Taylor. He is going to grow up, now thanks to you, to do great things for Christianity. That is why God sent me here to protect him. It was imperative that he not die in this incident today."

"So what would have happened if I wouldn't have been here? What would have happened if that kid would have died?"

"That was never in question. I knew you were going to be here. All that matters now is that he is ok. Things are going to be ok for you now too. God owes you big time. Because of your act of kindness and bravery you will now be rewarded by Him. You will now have the power to make whatever you want to happen, come true. Be careful though, because there can be consequences to your power."

"Well, right now all I want is for this pain in my head to go away."

My eye lids began to feel oppressed. Everything went black.

Chapter 2
Dream

I opened my eyes and found myself in my bed, back in my apartment. My heart was racing. I had dreamt the whole thing, that much was obvious. But it felt so real. All of the images in my head were so vivid. I could still picture everything as clearly as if I were just there. The kid in the middle of the street, the child across the road, the child again only this time standing over my sprawled out body; it was all right there in my head. The pictures were as clear to me as if I had been looking at them in albums my whole life. I remembered the pain that I had felt in my head. I'd never felt such a pain before. Literally, I had never felt such pain. That's because it never happened. My head felt fine now and pain like that just doesn't go away.

I looked over at my alarm clock. 4:30. I didn't need to be up for another hour. I laid my head back down to try to get some more sleep and forget about this silly dream, but I had no such luck. I was wide awake now. I didn't really feel tired at all. My body seemed well rested so there was no need to fight it. I got up and headed for the shower.

The steaming hot water felt so good against my cold, rejuvenated body. My head was full of worries and doubts but this magical hot water seemed to wash it all away. Momentarily at least, because as soon as I twisted the knob to off they were right there waiting on me.

I remembered the thoughts I was having during my dream, before it got all crazy. I had been used to hating my job and feeling like I was wasting my life, I felt like that every day. I was so used to feeling that way that it really didn't even bother me so much. Now that I had come to grips with the fact that I hated my life, it was actually becoming easier to enjoy.

But now the feeling was getting more intense. It was not enjoyable this morning at all. I could feel my face getter hotter as I dried my hair.

I threw the towel to the floor and started to storm out of the room. It would have been easier if the towel wouldn't have wrapped around my feet and made me fall on my face. I picked the towel up and stuffed it into the bathroom trashcan. Who needs so many towels anyways?

I sat in my Lazyboy waiting for this anger to dissipate as a pot of coffee brewed in the kitchen. I tried to think about all the good things in my life, in hopes of a cheer up. That just made me angrier when I couldn't think of anything. I didn't have a girlfriend, or really any prospects. I have distanced myself from all my old high school friends to the point where I'm not in contact with any of them anymore. I didn't like anyone I worked with, so no friends there. The only people I really talked to where the string of one night stands I drug back to my apartment night after night. Remembering back on some of my past sexual conquests did manage to bring a smirk to my face, but it was short lived.

I poured myself a cup of coffee and sat back down, this time feeling a little better. The caffeine seemed to be calming my nerves. I had been wrong before. I did have a friend. His name was Maxwell House. He always seemed to make me feel better when I was down.

It was still early and I had a while before I needed to get ready for work. It had been months since I'd been up early enough to watch a little bit of news in the morning. When I turned on the TV, the local news was just beginning.

"Stay tuned for the 5 o'clock evening news."

5 o'clock evening news? That must have been a mistake. There's no way I had over slept that much. My dad would have been here beating down my door. I walked over to the window to raise the blinds for confirmation. What I got instead was a surprise. The sun came beaming into the room.

I started to panic. I had never missed a day of work before. Not to mention I was just promoted. I imagined how this was going to go over with my dad, and none of the scenarios ended up nicely for me. I took a deep breath, braced myself, picked up the phone and began dialing his number. Before I could finish dialing, the commercials ended and what I heard next made me drop the phone to the ground.

"Tonight's top story: Local man saves life of young local boy!"

"Local hero Jaycin Smith was caught here by a store surveillance camera running into the middle of the street and pushing the unaware Daniel Taylor out of the way from an out of control, sliding SUV. Both parties escaped incident. The local hero was unavailable for comment. Our own Stacy Michaels caught up with the young boy, Daniel Taylor."

"Daniel, how are you feeling?"

"I really feel fine. Right now I'm just glad that someone was there to push me out of the way."

"Have you had a chance yet to talk to the man who saved your life?"

"No. He left really soon after. Someone told me his dad was on his way to work and seen him and took him home."

"Do you plan on trying to reach him at some point?"

"Yes. I really would like to thank him in person."

"Thank you, Daniel."

The story hadn't been over for ten seconds when my cell phone started ringing. It was dad.

"Hello."

"Hey son. I just saw the video of you on the news. I wanted to check on you and make sure you were still doing ok. You had a really close call back there."

"Yea I did, didn't I. You know, I wasn't really sure it had even happened until I seen it on the news. When I woke up I thought it was a dream."

"Well, it wasn't a dream, Hero!"

He chuckled after calling me Hero but I didn't. The realization was just hitting me. It wasn't a dream. Oh my God it wasn't a dream!

Chapter 3
Realization

If saving the kid was real, then it all had to be real.

The young screaming child was sent by God to have me save Daniel. I now have some mystical powers to make my wildest fantasies come true. These are things that must be true if any of it is.

I dropped to my knees from this realization, and I sighed loudly.

Why would God give me a power like this? I never went to church, argued in his favor, or spent my nights reading the Bible. Why not give it to someone more deserving? A priest perhaps, or a missionary.

As I was thinking about how I didn't deserve this, another thought crossed my mind. Maybe I don't have this power. Maybe I bumped my head so hard I just started seeing things.

I jumped up from my knees. There was only one way to know for sure whether or not I had this great gift. I would have to test it out.

I ran to the bedroom and changed out of the work clothes I had pointlessly put on just a short time ago. I slipped in to some more casual attire, grabbed my wallet and was ready to make my way into the city.

As I walked along the still snowy sidewalks, my mind was jumbled. What would I try first? Should I try something small or go for something major right off the bat.

The snow somewhat distracted me from these thoughts. The white flakes filled the evening sky with a beauty that would be hard to capture on a canvas. The falling snow made me think back to earlier in the day. How could something so lovely come so close to causing something so horrible? Nevertheless, I loved it and wished there would be more of it.

Just as the thought had escaped my mind the flakes started to come down harder. Did I do that or was it just a coincidence?

The frosty winter air was giving me a chill so I ducked into a coffee shop. The place was filled with all sorts of people. You had your groups of friends who were meeting up for coffee and you had your people who were stopping in for a steaming hot cup of joe after work. There was even on guy who looked to be working. This guy seemed to be getting under a lot of people's skin. He was alone at a table for four with folders spread everywhere as he typed away on his laptop.

I was standing in line waiting on my pumpkin spice latte, when I saw a group of guys ask the busy man if they could borrow a couple of chairs.

"This is my table. Those are my chairs. If you bother me again I'll give you one, but it will be across your face."

His rude response appalled me.

I thought someone should put that guy in his place. He wasn't using those chairs and the guys asked very nicely. There was no need for that kind of response. A thought crept into my mind. Maybe I can be the one to do something about it. I thought of a few different ways I could get him back but I decided on the one that would give me the most entertainment.

"Oh Shit!" He screamed out in pain. "Fuck it burns!"

I watched the man scream like a little girl as the hot coffee fell from the table and landed on his lap. He seemed to be in agony but I didn't try to fight back my smile. Neither did a lot of other people as laughter began to fill the coffee shop.

The man let out a few more obscenities, this time at the people who were laughing at him. That just made the people laugh harder.

I was still smiling too, but not for the same reason. I had wished that his coffee fall from the table and burn him and that is what happened. I wished for more snow and it started coming down harder. What the child had promised was true. I had a great new power.

Even though I was nearly a hundred percent sure that this power was real and not just a couple of coincidences, I wanted to try it out one more time to be certain.

The barista handed me my latte and I left the coffee shop and all the laughing patrons behind. After one sip of the latte, the chill that had entered my body was no longer anywhere to be found.

The streets were filled with children playing and adults admiring the beautiful snow. I wanted to take it all in myself so I found a nice bench to sit on while I finished my hot beverage.

I had been so stressed earlier this morning. My life was shit and I knew it. I felt none of that now, less than twenty four hours later. I had never felt more relaxed as I sat on that bench. Life felt good to me now.

As I sat on that bench, feeling great about life, I heard something that sent chills down my spine. It was the scream of a young child. My first thought was, Oh no. Not Again.

I flew off the bench and ran in the direction the scream came from. I heard another scream as I got closer to the edge of a building. The screams seemed to come from just around the corner.

I turned the corner to find three older kids pelting a younger child with snow balls. The child who was being hit by the snow balls was now curled up, defenseless against the wall. The three older kids were laughing as they hurled more snow balls as hard as they could.

I wished for something to stop this flogging.

You could hear a large gust of wind but in the alley you couldn't feel it. Moments later a massive amount of snow came pouring down from the roof knocking the three older boys down and covering them in snow.

I ran over to the younger child, who was spared from the avalanche, and helped him to his feet.

The younger child's face was blood red and there were tears frozen on his cheeks. I told him to run home. He took off running and made it home safe. I'm sure of it because I wished it to be true.

The other three boys started to make their way out of the large pile of snow. When the first one stuck his head out of the pile, I popped him in the face with a snowball.

"Ow!" He screamed. "What did you do that for?"

"If I find any of you picking on that kid again, I'll make you regret it for the rest of your lives," I threatened with a harsh tone.

None of the kids said a word. I could see from their faces they were frightened. They were also shivering from being covered in the snow.

As I turned to leave I decided that I'd had enough excitement for one day. I went back to my apartment and called it a night.

Chapter 4
Media

I was awoken by the irritating sound of the buzzer going off in my apartment. Someone was here to see me, but it was eight o' clock in the morning. I have no friends and my parents always call first.

My curiosity got the best of me. I rolled out of bed and walked over to the intercom.

"Yes? Who is it?" I asked in a barely audible, just woke up voice.

The voice of a young kid came out of my intercom speaker. "It's Daniel Taylor, sir. The boy you saved yesterday."

I was caught off guard. I knew he wanted to see me, but how did he find me so quickly? "Oh. Come on up." There was a hint of surprise in my voice.

I buzzed him in and threw on the first bit of clothes I could find—a pair of basketball shorts and a dirty white t-shirt.

I had just pulled the dirty shirt over my head when I heard a knock on my door. I rushed over to open the door, stubbing my toe on a chair and letting out an obscenity or two on the way.

There in the doorway stood the young lad from yesterday. I recognized him instantly. I didn't, however, recognize the attractive, statuesque woman who was accompanying him.

"Hello Mr. Smith!" Daniel said with excitement.

Introductions were made. The older woman with Daniel was his mother, as I had expected. I invited them in for drinks. He and his mother spent the next half hour thanking me profusely. I shrugged the whole incident off and credited instincts rather than heroism.

I could tell Daniel was a good kid. He was dressed very proper and had exquisite manners. I'm guessing he picked all that up from his mother. I spent a lot of my attention on her. She was very proper. She sat straight up in her chair, crossed her legs like a lady, and spoke with eloquence. There was no wedding ring on her finger, which I noticed within the first five seconds of seeing her, so I doubt he picked up these actions from his father.

They thanked me some more and then they left. I was sad to see them go, at least her anyways. I thought about how beautiful she was and how I would love to run in to her again someday. Seconds later there was a knock at my door.

It was Daniel's mother, only this time she was alone.

"Would you like to go out for dinner with us tonight?" she asked graciously.

"Oh, I wouldn't want to impose," I said, trying to keep from smiling. Would she be back if I hadn't wished to see her again?

"It would be no imposition at all. We would love to have you join us," she persisted.

"Well, I'd love to join you then," I said, no longer able to keep the smile from stretching across my face.

We arranged to meet at Barley's at seven o' clock tonight for pizza and some drinks.

I was extremely pleased with the situation, until I walked past a mirror. I looked like a fucking hobo. Was she just asking me out to dinner out of pity? If I seen someone looking like I did, I would assume they couldn't afford a nice meal either. I got in the shower, disgusted with myself.

After the shower I sat in my chair in a daze, staring at the TV, but it was only white noise to me. I closed my eyes and drifted off.

A few hours later I reopened my eyes to the TV still running. I was well rested but I felt famished. I wanted some take out but I didn't feel like waiting for it. I got out of my chair to go to the kitchen to see what I had. I never made it to the fridge because there on the table were four cartons of the best smelling Chinese food my nose had ever came across.

I devoured the Chinese food. It was as good as it smelled. I was loving this new power, it was coming in extremely handy.

It was only noon and I was already feeling anxious about tonight. I didn't have anything else to do today so if I couldn't find something to do, this anxiety would drive me nuts. I wished it was later in the day.

I closed my eyes and opened them again a second later. The light that had, only seconds ago filled my apartment, was now gone. I checked the clock. It was six o' clock.

Determined to prove to Daniel's mother that I wasn't a bum, I wore my best suit. I also threw in a little hair gel and sprayed on some of my best cologne. On the way to the door, I passed by the same mirror I had passed earlier this morning. I was much more pleased this time.

As I left my apartment, a friendly woman at the door asked me where I was going. I told her, and we chatted for only a moment and then I had to leave.

When I arrived, Daniel and his mother were already seated. I was just about to sit down when I saw a television crew come rushing into the restaurant. Following behind them was the friendly lady from outside my apartment building. Now she was holding a microphone. She was a reporter and my dumb ass was so arrogant earlier that I just thought she was hitting on me.

I heard one of the crew say, "Hell Yea! He's having dinner with the boy. This is gonna be gold!"

I knew I had been setup. There was no running from it now. I sat down, whispered an apology to Daniel's mom, and waited for the ambush to begin.

She started with Daniel. "Daniel, I see you finally got the chance to meet your hero in person."

Daniel smiled but his mother spoke up for him. "He has and he's very happy about it but we're having dinner at the moment and he won't be answering any questions tonight."

When the reporter seen she would get nothing from Daniel she moved on to me. "So, Mr. Smith, how does it feel to be a hero?"

I said, as politely as I could, "It's very rewarding but I really can't talk to you guys right now. Thank you for coming though."

"I have a job to do and I'm not leaving until I get my interview," she said stubbornly.

I could see that there was going to be nothing I could do, so I excused myself from the table and said, "I'll answer your questions but not here. We have to go outside. It's rude and inappropriate to come in here and ruin everyone's dinner."

At this point I was highly pissed. I hadn't even had time to make myself comfortable before they busted in and ruined my evening.

Once outside I was determined to make them pay. I wished something would happen that would make them all go away.

Before the reporter could ask her first question, she began vomiting in the street. The other members of the crew began to follow suit. It was a disgusting, but very rewarding site.

Someone in the crew said, "They must have given us some bad food down at the station."

The reporter was about to say something to me but I interjected, "I think that maybe we should try this some other time. I'd hate to catch whatever you all seem to have."

I turned around and walked back towards Barley's with a smirk on my face. This time they didn't follow.

I sat back down at our table. I watched everyone staring at me in my peripherals. I apologized to Daniel and his mother once more, for the interruption.

Dinner was hard to enjoy with all the staring and talking about us. We ate as fast as we could, said our goodbyes, and went our separate ways.

It was a disappointing end to the evening but at least I had a little sweet justice with the television crew.

Chapter 5
Excitement

The television crew never came back to visit me. After the dinner fiasco, I was worried for a day or two, but each day they didn't show, I became a little more relaxed. My demeanor was reaching heights I wasn't sure existed.

The first thing that happened to lighten my mood was when my father called Sunday night to inform me I could take a couple weeks off work to recuperate from the incident. I hadn't thought of wishing for that yet, so the call came as a bit of a nice surprise.

Now that I didn't have to work for a while, I decided partying would be a nice treat for me.

The next few nights were a blur. It was hard to believe that one person could have this much fun. I spent night after night in club after club bringing home girl after girl. They were defenseless against my newfound power but it didn't make it any less fun.

I knew things were starting to get out of hand for me when I woke up next to a beautiful lady that any man would love to be with, yet I was disappointed. The thrill of bringing random girls home every night was starting to wear thin. I needed to turn the excitement up a notch.

The next night I went from bar to bar trying to find something to peak my interest. I was nearly at the point of giving up when I saw them.

My gazing caught the attention of one of the girls at the table. She smiled and I knew I had found my entertainment for the night.

I had never had a threesome before, but every guy wants to. The fact that they were twin sisters just put the icing on the cake. I walked over to the table and asked the ladies if they would like to accompany me back to my apartment. It's not hard to do this when the fear of rejection is gone.

I had a lot of fun that night but I knew the thrill wouldn't last. I would have to keep topping myself until I eventually hit a point I couldn't top.

The thought of reaching that point depressed me. The next night I decided to stay in and watch some University of Tennessee basketball on TV. If I was going to get to that point then I needed to pace myself.

The game was about to start when an idea struck me. I worked with a guy who was a huge University of Kentucky fan and that was who Tennessee was playing. I called him up and asked him if he wanted to put a wager on a game.

With a hundred dollars on the line, I kicked back with a cold one and began wishing for Tennessee to blow out Kentucky. It wasn't much of a contest but one thing did catch my eye. Tennessee's dance squad had some very attractive girls on it.

I knew hooking up with the whole dance squad would be hard to top, but my lack of self control didn't care. I wished for them to show up at my door.

The game had ended an hour ago and the girls still hadn't shown up. I was starting to doubt my powers when my buzzer sounded.

When they reached my door I asked them what made them end up at my place. The cute blonde in front answered, "We're tired of bars. We just wanted to ring a random buzzer and party with whoever answered the door."

Much alcohol was consumed and many other things happened that cannot be repeated.

When morning came the girls were all complaining of hangovers. I was magically, perfectly fine. At least I thought so.

I drank some coffee and watched some Sportscenter as the girls made their way out of my apartment. When the last one left I went to the bathroom to take a piss and a shower. As I tried to relieve myself of the coffee from this morning and the alcohol from the night before, I felt an extremely painful burning sensation. The pain brought me to my knees. I wished for it to go away.

The pain left and I got up, wondering which one of those bitches had given me a STD. I was going to wish something bad on whomever it was but when I turned around, I was met by the startling site of the young child who claimed to be Daniel's guardian angel.

He stood smirking against the wall. "Have fun last night?"

"Night, yes. Morning, not so much." I was feeling a little embarrassed because I knew this small, childlike figure knew what my night had consisted of.

His face took on a more serious appearance. "Look, I told you there would be consequences to your powers. We'll fix the one problem, but from now on you have to be a little more careful. Can you do that?"

"I'll do my best." I answered, face now red with shame and eyes looking at the ground, not worthy of looking him in the eyes.

The child didn't respond. When I looked up, he was gone.

"Little, sneaky bastard."

Chapter 6
Brittany

As I lay in my bed, thinking of how insane my life had become, I came to the conclusion that I needed to change. My life at the moment was exciting and fun, but I was going to destroy myself if I didn't calm down a little. I needed more stability in my life—I needed a girlfriend.

It had been a while since I had a serious relationship, but I was excited about the idea of dating. Of course, there was the one minor detail. Who was I going to date?

I knew with my power, it wouldn't be hard to find someone; the hard part would be finding someone I wanted to be with. I enjoyed the company of a woman for an hour or two, but I can't remember the last time I wanted to be around one for anything more than sex.

When I woke up the next morning my mind was made up. It was time I went on an all out search for a girlfriend.

I hit the streets early, hoping to find a nice woman on her way to work that I might be able to strike up a conversation with.

The first woman that caught my eye was a good looking brunette wearing a nice pant suit. She looked very professional and I find that extremely sexy. I wished for her to like me before I approached her to talk. I introduced myself, and as soon as she spoke I knew she wasn't the one. Her voice was painfully annoying. I would rather have someone beating me in the face with a hammer than to listen to her talk. It was like someone was scratching a blackboard with their finger nails. Before she could finish what she was saying, I turned and walked away.

I was slightly disappointed, but that was just a first attempt. There are thousands of women in this city; surely one of them would be bearable.

The next woman I decided to approach was another brunette, this one dressed very casually in blue jeans and a coat. She looked to be out doing some early shopping. She was pretty enough, and seemed nice enough too, but after five minutes of talking to her I was pretty sure she was the dumbest person on the planet. There wasn't one intelligent thing that came out of her mouth. It was obvious she had coasted her whole life on her good looks.

I decided to give up on the girlfriend search for a while and have some breakfast.

After breakfast, most of the women were either off to their jobs, or still at home in bed. If I was going to find a girlfriend now, I was going to have to wait until lunch time. I didn't feel like going back to my apartment so instead I went to the bookstore. I picked up a book by Mark Haddon called *The Curious Incident of the Dog in the Night-Time*. I bought the book and took it back to the coffee shop to read while I would await my future wife.

It had been a long time since I had sat down and read a book for enjoyment. It was a really good book. A little too good because when I managed to come out of my reading trance and look up, lunch time had already come and gone. I had missed another opportunity and my patience was beginning to wear thin.

I was just about to pick up my book and leave, when a beautiful blonde sat down at my table.

"Hey, how do you like the book?" She said with a voice that didn't want to make me kill myself.

"It's really good."

"It's my favorite book of all time," she said cheerfully, as she sat her stuff down and made herself comfortable.

"I'm Katherine." She reached out her hand for me to shake.

"I'm Jaycin. Nice to meet you." I took her hand in mine and instantly I could feel a definite connection.

We talked for close to an hour. She was smart, funny, and beautiful, and she was into me even though I hadn't used my powers on her even once. She was the person I had been looking for.

As the conversation was coming to a close, it was time for me to make my move.

"Would you like to have dinner with me sometime?" I asked, as bravely as I could manage.

"Yea! I'm not doing anything tonight." She pulled out a card with her contact information on it. "Call me later."

I took the card and promised I'd call. I stood there for a second and watched her leave. When she was gone, I bent down to get my stuff; then as I turned to leave I bumped into someone knocking them down and spilling their coffee. I reached down to help the lady up, and that's when I seen her.

When I was in high school I had the biggest crush on Brittany Love. She was the most beautiful girl I had ever seen, but I never had the courage to talk to her. Now, here I was helping her off the ground that I had just knocked her to. She was still as beautiful as ever. She had long, flowing red hair, long legs, pale skin (but not ghostly white), and a face that's beauty almost made you want to cry.

"I'm so sorry." I grabbed her hands and pulled her to her feet. "Please, let me get you another coffee."

"Oh, that's ok. Don't worry about...." She paused and started smiling. "Didn't I go to school with you?"

"Yea. I think you did." I said, hoping she didn't remember the loser I was back then.

Before this could get any worse, I wished she wouldn't be pissed at me for knocking her down, and also wished she would let me take her out to make up for it.

"Jaycin, right?"

I was shocked she remembered my name. "Yea. And you're Brittany?" I asked, already knowing I was right.

"Yea. Good to see you again!" She wrapped her arms around me and gave me a big hug.

We sat down at the closest table and began catching up. She said she was recently divorced; apparently they argued all the time. They never had any kids, so all of this was pointing to an opportunity for me. She also talked about seeing me on the news, and then began to tell me how brave I was.

I apologized once more for knocking her down and spilling her coffee. I asked her if she would let me take her to dinner tonight to properly make up for it.

She agreed.

The time we departed from each other's company until the time of our date just couldn't go by fast enough. It had been a while since my last "real" date, and the anxiety was killing me. There wasn't a thought that entered my mind that wasn't about my date with the lovely Brittany Love. I knew I had the power to make everything go well, but that would've taken all the fun and intrigue out of the date.

The Knoxville skyline was beautiful at night. Especially on a clear, cloudless night like it was that night. I met up with Brittany at the same coffee shop where I had brutally knocked her down earlier in the day. When I first seen her I wasn't sure what to do. Do I give her a hug? Kiss on the cheek? Am I supposed to hold her hand? Is this a friend date or a real date? These questions rushed into my mind almost sending me into a panic.

Luckily I didn't have to worry for long, because she ran in with a charming smile on her face, grabbed my hand, and said "let's go."

I made reservations at one of the nicest restaurants in town. I was worried that it might come off as me trying too hard, but she seemed very pleased with the choice. The conversation started out nice, but we quickly ran out of things to talk about and I could feel this date starting to slip away. I gave in to temptation and wished that she would think this was the best date of her life, and she would fall in love with me.

Not two seconds after I had made the wish she looked at me, smiled and grabbed my hand to hold. I was feeling pretty good about myself now, so I asked her if she wanted to dance.

Everyone was staring at us as we danced in the middle of the dining room. I was having too much fun for the staring to bother me. I was with the most beautiful girl in the world, they could stare all the wanted. When the song ended I made my move, going in for a kiss.

We kissed passionately. For a moment I forgot there were other people in the room. When the kiss ended there was a small round of applause from some of the other people in the restaurant. Normally I would have been embarrassed, but not tonight. I could tell Brittany wasn't embarrassed either, by the little curtsy and smile she gave as we walked back to our table.

I don't think our eyes left each others for the rest of dinner. We shared a desert—hot fudge sundae—and I asked her what she was going to do the rest of the night. She said, "I was just going to go back to my place, kick back and watch a movie." Then she smiled a devilish smile, "Do you wanna come back and join me?"

I smiled back. "Nah, I think I'll probably just go home and watch some TV or something."

Her eyes widened with surprise.

"I'm just kidding. Of course I'll join you."

If this night had lasted forever it wouldn't have been long enough. We sat on the couch to watch a movie, granted we weren't there for long before we made our way back to the bedroom, but I could have sat next to her on the couch for the rest of my life and been perfectly content. I knew, from that point on, I never wanted to be apart from her.

The next morning I woke up holding her nude, goddess like body next to mine. We spent hours that day just lying there next to each other. It was the best day of my life.

Chapter 7
Consequences

It had been weeks since my first date with Brittany and everything in my life was aces; it was hard to imagine that I wasn't dreaming. Waking up to her face was better than anything I could have dreamt up on my own.

After staring at her and watching her sleep for a while, I climbed out of bed and walked outside into a beautiful morning. Everything had been beautiful lately. Every time I walked by a mirror and caught a glimpse of myself, I had a huge smile on my face. I was happier now, than I could ever remember myself being before.

When I got upstairs, Brittany was no longer in the bed. I stopped breathing momentarily but resumed again when I heard the shower running. I was about to hop back in bed and wait for her to get out, when I heard a noise coming from the night stand. I walked over to where I thought the sound had come from. The sound began again and this time I was there to see what the cause was. It was Brittany's phone vibrating against the hard wood of the night stand.

The face of the phone was lit up and read "one new text message." Curiosity got the best of me. I opened the phone and came across a text conversation that she had been having with her mom during the time that I had spent outside.

Text Messages

Brittany:Hey. You up?

Mom:Hi! What are you doin?

Brittany:Laying in bed. Jaycin just walked outside.

Mom:How are things going with you two kids?

Brittany:Everything is great! My only worry is, he's been out of work for a while now and if things are going to keep getting more serious I want to know he's going to be able to take care of me. Right now it feels like I'm going to have to take care of him.

Mom:If you love each other it'll work out.

Brittany:I do love him but I want a man, not a charity case.

Mom:Well give it some time. Maybe he'll get it together.

Brittany:I hope so.

Mom:Me too. Ok hunny, have a good day.

I sat the phone down on the night stand and looked up in the mirror. The smile I had been walking around with for weeks was now gone. The woman I loved thought I was a loser.

The door to the bathroom opened up behind me. In the mirror I could see Brittany standing behind me, wearing nothing but a towel. Even that couldn't bring a smile back to my face.

"Is something wrong?"

"No, just trying to figure out what I'm going to do today."

"I can think of a few things," she said with a sinister grin just before dropping her towel to the floor.

A few hours later I rolled out of the bed for the second time. The fact that Brittany thought I was a loser was still engraved in my mind. I know I could make her stay with me if I wanted to, but I wanted her to want to. I needed to be able to make a secure and happy life for her. I needed to grow up.

I decided to take a walk downtown to clear my head and come up with a plan. Not too long into my journey I saw my answer. It came to me in the form of a huge billboard that read: Play Powerball. Jackpot Now At 126 million. All I needed to do was wish to be a millionaire. Then if I didn't have a job,it would be because I was rich, not because I was a loser.

I made the wish. I stopped right there where I was, closed my eyes and said, "I wish I was a millionaire."

I opened my eyes and started looking for a gas station.

A few minutes later I was standing in line, about to have the key to making my future wife very happy.

THE REWARD FROM ABOVE

I had the clerk pick my lotto numbers randomly. I gave him a dollar, took my ticket and went back home.

Brittany was gone when I got back. This time I was expecting it. She was going to her mom's house (probably to talk about me some more). That's ok though, because when she gets back I'll have a winning lottery ticket to surprise her with.

I waited around for a couple hours waiting for them to give out the winning numbers. I was pretty sure I knew what they would be, but I was still excited all the same.

Disappointment ran thru my veins when the numbers on the TV didn't match the numbers on my ticket. It was the first time I had wished for something that didn't come true.

I plopped down in a chair and contemplated what could have possibly gone wrong.

A knock on the door broke my concentration. Brittany had a key so I knew it wasn't her, and I wasn't expecting anyone else. I jumped up and ran to the door.

When I opened the door I knew something was wrong. A tall, thick man, wearing a policeman's uniform, was standing in the door way.

"Can I help you, officer?" The fear in my voice wasn't hard to ascertain.

"Yes, you can. I'm Officer Sheppard. I'm looking for Jaycin Smith."

"I'm Jaycin Smith. Did I do something wrong, officer?"

"Oh, no sir!" He looked down at his hands appearing to be nervous now.

"I'm afraid I have some news for you." Still looking down, avoiding eye contact with me.

"News?"

"Yes sir. I regret to inform you that your parents were in an accident just a short while ago."

"An accident? Are they ok? Where are they?" I was freaking out. The more I freaked out the more nervous the officer became.

"There at UT Medical Center, but I'm sorry sir. They didn't make it."

"Didn't make it?" Tears started to fill my eyes. "What the fuck do you mean they didn't make it!?" I had dropped down to my knees, in shock.

The officer reached down to help me to my feet. "I'm really sorry, sir. I can give you a ride if you'd like. Anything you need, just ask and it's done."

I was on my feet now, crying into the officer's shoulder. "No, thank you. I'll drive myself," I managed to mumble out between sobs.

I called Brittany on the way to the hospital. She was waiting on me at the doors when I arrived. We hugged a long, heartfelt hug. She was crying but there were no more tears left for me to cry. The receptionist told us where we should go. Seeing their lifeless bodies laying there on a table was more that I could handle. The tears that I thought had ran dry, started flowing again. I was crying so hard, my face hurt.

After identifying the bodies, we went back to my place. There was a list of stuff that needed taken care of, but I wasn't in the mood to deal with any of it. Brittany called everyone that needed to be notified, and took care of making all the funeral arrangements.

I didn't get out of bed again until it was time to meet with the lawyers to go over my parent's will. I didn't bother showering; I just threw on some dirty clothes that were lying in the floor.

I pretty much knew what to expect. I had no brothers or sisters, so I knew I was going to get everything, which wouldn't be much. A nice house but not much else. My parents weren't poor, but they weren't really rich either.

The lawyer started off by telling me how sorry he was for my loss. I thanked him but I couldn't help wondering how many times he'd said that before.

"Can we just get down to business? I don't really want to be here so if you can speed it along…"

"Yes. I completely understand. Let's get down to business. You'll get your parent's house of course. There was only liability coverage on the car, so no money from that. We've obtained all the bank records and the total cash comes out to a little more than twelve thousand dollars."

"Ok, well thank you for everything."

"Wait. There's one more thing. They both had an accidental death insurance policy. You'll receive one million dollars for each of them."

I sat there in shock for a moment. I couldn't come up with any words to say.

The lawyer broke the silence. "I know losing both your parents is a hard thing to cope with and you may not appreciate this money now, but you will be a millionaire. You're set for life now."

He was right. I was a millionaire. I was set up for life. However, he was wrong about one thing. Coping with my parent's death would be easy compared to coping with the fact of knowing I was the one who killed them.

Chapter 8
Guilt

Everyone I knew got in touch with me over the next couple days. I wished they would just leave me alone. I didn't have anything to say to anyone. I'm sure I came off as rude, but they probably just chalked it up to sadness over losing my parents.

The truth is I wasn't feeling sad at all. I was angry. No, furious is more like it. I murdered my parents. Not in the way that would have me put in prison, but I killed them just the same. And for what? Some money? I couldn't even enjoy the money. I hadn't spent one dime of it, yet.

The only person left in this world that I cared about was Brittany and I couldn't stand to look at her. In my head, I had started to place a lot of the blame on her. IF she wasn't thinking of leaving me for not being able to support her, then I wouldn't have been worrying about money in the first place.

I started spending more and more time on my own, away from her. I would go to the movies alone to clear my head and help me forget about what I had done. The problem with movies, however, was it only lasted for an hour or two. As soon as I walked out of the theatre, the pain would hit me again. I needed a more permanent vacation from the pain. That's when I turned to alcohol.

When a movie ended after those two hours I had to leave, but in a bar I could stay as long as I wanted. The more beer I would drink, the less pain I felt, until eventually I would drink so much I felt nothing.

Brittany and I grew further apart by the day. She spent all her time at work and at her mom's house, while I spent all my time getting as drunk as I could.

It took me a while to realize that I had a serious problem. My epiphany moment came late on a Friday night while I was in Nashville, visiting an old friend. I never bothered to tell Brittany that I was going out of town.

My friend knew I was feeling down so he decided to take me to a strip club. It actually did help me feel better at first. I mean, what guy doesn't like watching girls take off their clothes, and making it rain like Pac Man Jones. No, my moment came later on.

I purchased a table dance from a sexy blonde with fake hair and fake boobs. After the dance she grabbed my hand and drug me back to the VIP area. I was really starting to enjoy myself at this point. She threw me down on the black leather couch, climbed on top of me and kissed me. The kissing went on for a few minutes before it hit. Thoughts ran through my head. "What the fuck are you doing? Your dream girl is at home, probably missing you right now, and you're here about to fuck some dirty whore. What would your parents think?"

I shoved the stripper out of my lap.

"I'm sorry. I have to go."

I tossed her a hundred dollar bill and left. I didn't bother saying goodbye to my friend. Nothing mattered to me now except getting home to my beautiful girl.

Chapter 9
Piling On

I drove home as fast as the car would go. I would say it was a miracle I didn't get a ticket but it wasn't. I made sure to wish all the cops out of my path.

It felt like a huge weight had been lifted off me. I no longer felt that resentment toward the one person I had left on this earth. All that was left to do now was to make it right with her.

I knew once I seen her I would owe her an apology. I wanted to do better than that though. Once I finally made it back to Knoxville I made a few stops, I bought a dozen roses and the best chocolates I could find. I also got her a card and wrote her a sweet poem inside. When you've been as big of an ass as I had been of late, you don't look for reconciliation empty handed.

Anticipation was replaced by disappointment as I pulled into my driveway. Brittany's car was not there. I went inside to see if I could find some sort of clue as to where she might be. There were no notes, no messages of any kind waiting for me.

I took it upon myself to go to the only other place where I could imagine her being; her mom's house. Once I got, back in the car and started on my way, my spirit lifted back up. Less than twenty-four hours ago the thought of seeing her horrified me, now it was the only thing I wanted.

The ten minute drive seemed to take hours. My hopes were shot down again when I seen that her car was not in this driveway either. Her mom's car, on the other hand, was in the driveway. I pulled in behind the shiny, black Dodge Charger. Before I could get to the door to ring the doorbell,

Brittany's mother, Rachel, had her arms around my neck hugging the life out of me.

"Oh, Jaycin. It's so good to see you!" Her arms were still wrapped around my neck, hugging the life out of me.

"It's really good to see you too, Ms. Love." I actually, really was glad to see her.

"How have you been, Hun?"

"Not so good, lately. I think I'm finally coming out of my funk, though."

"That's good. So what brings you down this way?"

"Actually, I just got in from out of town and was looking for Brittany. Do you happen to know where she is?"

"Yea. I just talked to her a little while ago. She said she was going to your old apartment to pick up a few more things."

"Oh. I didn't know there was anything left out there. Well I guess I'll go over there and see if I can catch her; see if she needs some help or something."

"Ok sweetie. You and Britt get back down here and see me soon."

"We will. Bye Ms. Love." This time I gave her the big hug.

I couldn't wait any longer; I had to see her now. If I waited for her to show up at home it wouldn't be the same as me tracking her down and surprising her. I thought she might even find it romantic.

I thought I was about to be disappointed once more when I didn't see her car in the parking lot. I thought I may have just missed her, and my opportunity at surprising her on top of that. I went on up to the apartment to see what else we hadn't moved out yet. I put the key into the keyhole, unlocked the door and went inside. I brought the chocolates, card and flowers up with me just in case she was there. As I sat the gifts down on the kitchen table, I heard a crash come from the bedroom and then I heard Brittany scream. I ran to the door to see if she was ok. The door was open and there was my girl, laying on the floor, and a strange man lying on top of her.

I didn't waste any time getting out of there. For the second time in months my heart was shattered. I didn't see any way of repairing it this time.

Chapter 10
Anger Management

I turned back toward the apartments, my mind filled with rage. I raised my left arm and pointed to the apartments and said, "I wish this building would burn to the ground." I closed my eyes.

When I re-opened my eyes, the sky had darkened. Loud, crashing thunder serenaded everyone who was near. People started gathering around, looking at the sky in awe. There were whispers of storms and tornadoes, and some people, who must not have known where they were, mentioned hurricanes. Then, just as the thunder had subsided, one bolt came striking down from the sky.

The apartment building lit up like a Christmas tree.

The sky cleared up instantly, but the streets were now replete with panic. People in the apartments had their windows open, screaming for help from the people below. I looked up at my old apartment window. Brittany was in the window screaming with the rest. Her eyes caught my stare and her screams stopped. I turned my back to her and walked away—leaving my whole life behind me, burning in flames.

I never once looked back as I got in my car and drove away. Innocent people were paying for her mistake, and it didn't bother me in the least. It gave me this great sense of power, like nothing, or no insignificant being could keep me from doing anything I pleased. This, and the combination of the rage running thru my veins, didn't bode well for anyone who crossed my path.

As I was driving to nowhere, I came to a park. The sight of two lovers on a park bench had grabbed my attention. I was in no mood for love. A nearby jogger with a beast of a German shepherd was running along a trail. I made a wish, and then I enjoyed the sight of the large dog attacking the couple on the bench. Their shrieks and cries were music to my ears.

I didn't stick around to see how bad it got. I needed to go around and take out more of my anger out on unsuspecting bystanders.

As I drove out of the park, a car cut me off. I followed the driver closely and discovered it was a woman who was talking on her cell phone. We were coming up on an intersection in about seventy-five yards. I wished that she wouldn't make it thru without getting smashed by another vehicle.

As I finished up my wish I noticed her phone was no longer attached to her ear, and she looked to be fumbling around trying to get something out of the floorboard. I started to slow down, getting further away from her the closer we got to the intersection. As she reached again, into the floorboard of her car, the light that was green suddenly changed to red; no yellow light ever appeared. The next time she looked up it was too late. A large Ford truck barreled into the side of her small sports car, sending it rolling down the highway.

I drove away from the wreckage, but was unsure about what to do next. I wasn't ready to go home. Everything there reminded me of her. What I needed to do was bring about more destruction.

An idea struck me. I drove to one of the worst parts of Knoxville. It was getting late now, so it shouldn't have been too hard to find some trouble. I parked on the side of the road, grabbed my dad's old pistol out of the glove box, and got out of the car ready to face the evils that lurked in the night.

I walked up and down the streets, down the shadiest alleys, anywhere I thought there might be trouble, but I couldn't find any. I decided to try to entice the criminals a little bit.

I pulled out my wallet from my back pocket and took out a bunch of cash. Now, I was walking up and down the streets, counting money as I went. It didn't take long to get the reaction that I was so desperately seeking.

As I passed one of the many creepy alleys, a man crept out behind me. He said, "Stop!" in a quiet but stern, commanding voice.

I turned around, stared him in the face and didn't say a word. In his same voice he said, "Put the money on the ground and walk away and you'll live through this.

I did as the man said. I laid the money on the ground and then took two steps backwards, never taking my eyes of his. He reached down, picked up the money, and then rose with a giant smile on his face. When he saw that I didn't walk away, his smile turned into a look of confusion.

"I thought I told you to walk away, son."

Without a word, I raised the gun from my waistline and shot the man in the forehead. I grabbed my money from his hands and started looking for another criminal.

Once again, it didn't take very long. This time I heard someone walking close behind me, but I hadn't passed any alleys. I wasn't sure where the person had come from. That made me a little leery. If he was sneaky enough to get behind me without my noticing, then he might be pretty dangerous.

I turned around sharply to catch a glimpse of the predator. At first I saw no one, but then I looked down, and there he was. It was the guardian angel again; tears were streaming down his face.

"What have you become?"

"Your God made me this way. I was normal once. I didn't have a lot going for me, but all I have now is heartbreak."

"God didn't do this to you. Your selfishness did. He gave you a reward that most people would relish, and you squandered it away."

"I don't need this." Then I closed my eyes and said, "I wish you would go away."

I opened my eyes and he was gone.

All of his talk took me out of my destructive mood; now I just felt like a huge waste of life. I thought about what would be next for me. I still couldn't go home. I had nothing left. My life was basically over now. If I went on living I would just be bringing pain to other people.

I drove around trying to come up with some kind of plan. The only thing I could come with was wishing I was dead. I didn't particularly care for that plan. The way I'd acted lately, I didn't want any part of however God would decide to kill me. The only reasonable thing to do would be to kill myself.

When I came to this realization, I stopped the car. It was the only thing that made sense. I stepped out of the car and lay down on the hood. I pulled out my dead father's gun and placed the barrel softly against my temple. I closed my eyes.

I opened my eyes again. I couldn't bring myself to pull the trigger. If I was going to do this I was going to have to find another way.

I got back into my car and started driving once more. I took a winding road that led from the park, up to the top of a large ridge.

Once I reached the top, I didn't even think about it. I drove straight off the ridge. Not very far into the long trip down, the car slammed into a large oak tree. Everything went black.

Chapter 11
New Start

When I woke up, the first thing I noticed was the blood; there was so much blood. I couldn't move any part of my body except for my eyelids. I didn't feel any pain, but I wasn't sure how long I'd been out, my body had gone numb.

I glanced around as best I could, which wasn't a lot since I couldn't move my head. There was lots of broken glass lying around me. I could tell I was still in my car and that it was now lying on its top. I could also tell that I was now in the back seat. I couldn't be sure, but I felt like I was at the bottom of the ridge now. The car was lying flat, not tilted like it would have been if it were on a hill. I started feeling really weak. Holding my eyes open became increasingly more challenging. I eventually succumbed to the wariness and closed my eyes.

Off in the distance I could hear the sound of sirens. It seemed to be coming towards me quickly because the siren grew louder and louder by the second. I tried to open my eyes at the hope of catching a glimpse of some emergency lights; but it was to no avail.

The sirens kept getting closer. Once I heard the doors open and close, I knew they were there for me. I could hear people talking now. It sounded like two guys. I heard one guy say, "Oh shit! There's no way anyone survived that."

I felt my body shifting. They were dragging me out of the car now.

"Is he dead?"

"Hold on. Let me check his pulse."

As the guy was checking my pulse he asked, "Can you hear me? Squeeze my hand if you can hear me."

I wanted to answer him but I couldn't. The words just wouldn't go from my brain to my mouth. I tried squeezing his hand but that didn't work either.

"He's got a pulse but it's really weak, plus he's lost a whole lot of blood. He's not going to make it. He'll be dead in minutes."

His words sparked something inside me. I knew I was hurt bad, but I never thought I was going to die. I thought dying was what I wanted, but hearing it come out of his mouth, I felt frightened. I didn't want to die. No matter how bad my life was, I just wasn't ready for it to end. If I was to die now, then my life would end with what was without a doubt, the worst day of my life. I didn't want to go out like that. I wished to not be hurt anymore.

Seconds later I felt some pressure on my neck. My eyes opened to see a man standing over me, pushing two fingers into the side of my neck. His eyes suddenly widened, "Now his pulse is racing!"

He looked down at my face and then jumped back in shock.

"You're awake!"

"Yea. Thanks for all your help but I think I can manage from here."

"No way! We're taking you to the hospital. You're hurt really bad and lost a lot of blood. Don't move. We have to get the stretcher."

He took off running as fast as he could toward the ambulance.

I got to my feet and started dusting myself off.

"Fuck! I can't believe he's able to stand up!"

"He's what?" The man who had been checking my pulse sounded very displeased. "Lay back down, now! You're going to hurt yourself worse than you already are!"

Ignoring his orders, I started to look around. My car was DESTROYED! There were parts of the roof touching the floor board. The driver's side mirror was barely hanging on. I walked up to it and kicked it the rest of the way off. It had a crack running thru the glass part, but I was still able to pick it up and use it to give myself a look over. If I had any cuts or bruises, they were gone now. The blood, however, was not gone. I was covered in it.

A hand landed on my shoulder. "Look, I'm not trying to be a jerk here, but you really need to let us take you to the hospital."

"I'll make a deal with you. You give me a physical, and then, if you still think I need to go to the hospital, I will."

Before we started the physical he gave me a bottle of water. I drank a little, but used most of it to wash some of the blood off me.

He checked me very thoroughly, but couldn't find anything seriously wrong with me.

"You're covered in so much blood, yet I can't find a scratch on you."

"I'm a quick healer," I jokingly said to him. "So, we done here?"

"I still think you need to come with us to the hospital."

"Fuck you! I'm not going anywhere."

"But we had a deal." He started inching closer to me.

"Yea, but you didn't find anything wrong."

"That wasn't the deal," he was right but I didn't care.

"If you come any closer, you'll be the one needing to go to the hospital."

He stopped and gave me a serious look. We stared at each other for a moment, and then I cracked a smile. All three of us broke out into a light hearted laughter.

"Well, I guess I couldn't find anything wrong with you. If I hadn't seen you earlier, I would think you were fine."

"Does that mean I can leave?"

"Yea, you're free to go." We shook hands and then the two guys got into the ambulance and went on about their business.

Not long after the ambulance pulled out of sight, I left the wreckage behind. Even though I was out of a car and out of a place to go, I felt a sense of relief. I think a near death experience will do that to you. It puts everything else into perspective.

I was getting a second chance at life now, and this time I was going to do it right. No more selfish wishes for me. That got me nowhere except bloody and lifeless at the bottom of a ridge. This time around I was going to make a difference.

It wasn't too far of a walk before I got back to some kind of civilization. I walked into the first motel I could find and got a room. I couldn't go in many places covered in blood so I wished for all my clothes at my house to be in my closet. I hopped in the shower to clean myself the rest of the way up. When I got out, all my clothes were there hanging in the closet, so I got dressed; it was nice to be clean and have on clean clothes again.

I ordered some take out. I hadn't had any food in I don't know how long. After scarfing the food down, I lay down in bed and began trying to come up with things I could do to become a better person.

I woke up around noon of the next day. While lying in bed last night, I decided the best way to start being better was to try to help people who couldn't help themselves.

I called a taxi and had the driver take me to the bank. First thing I did was have them cancel Brittany's debit card so that she would have no way to touch my money. After that had been done, I took out a little bit of cash. I left the bank and started searching for a new vehicle. I wasn't looking for any normal car or truck; I had something different in mind.

When I found what I was looking for I went back to pay the cab driver. I gave him a very nice tip, then went back to get the keys to my new box truck.

I took my new truck to a grocery store and loaded it up with five thousand dollars worth of non-perishable foods.

The local homeless shelter was surprised but very grateful for my delivery. I spent an hour or so talking to the person who ran the downtown shelter. He told me how some of the homeless have to sleep on the floor because they don't have enough beds, and even if they did have enough, they didn't have enough room to put the beds in.

It was nice to talk with someone who was helping these people and asking for nothing in return. All he wanted was to help make these people's lives just a little bit better. On my way out I stopped, pulled out my wallet, and cut the guy a check for a hundred grand. I made him promise he would use the money to build a new addition and buy some extra beds. He smiled gratefully and assured me that's exactly what the money would go for. He even invited me back for weekly status updates.

Chapter 12

Super

Helping out the homeless had me feeling really good about myself. The question I asked myself now was, "What's next?"

There were still people out there who needed help, and I could help them. The problem I was having was figuring out who to help. I wanted to help everyone, but I couldn't be everywhere at once. Then I got an idea.

I may not be able to be everywhere, but I could make myself be able to get wherever I was going faster. What I needed were some super powers. I could build myself into a real life super hero. I could make myself be able to fly, be stronger, and have bullet proof skin, be the kind of super hero that people read about in comics. Only I wouldn't have any super villains trying to take me down, and I could build myself to have no flaws. That's exactly what I did.

Now that I had superpowers I needed a way to find out when someone needed help. I wasn't taking orders from a secret government branch or looking for a light in the sky that the mayor was shining. I had to find these people on my own.

After debating a while on whether or not I should get a cool costume (I chose not to), I went to Best Buy and bought myself a police scanner.

When I got back to the motel, I plugged in my new partner. It didn't take long for him to come through for me.

"Attention all units in downtown area. Black Cadillac Escalade refusing to pull over. Currently going north on Cherry Street. Unit looking for backup in pursuit."

I didn't have a chance to test out any of my new powers yet, but this opportunity was too good to pass up. I took off running out the door and leapt off the third floor balcony. I really should have tested out the flying first, because it didn't work out so well that first time; didn't work at all actually. I ended up crashing through the window of someone's shiny red BMW.

I tried a few different take offs as I ran down the street with my new super speed. It took a couple of tries, but I finally figured it out. I shot through the sky like I was Superman, only I wouldn't have dropped out of the sky if it started raining kryptonite.

Up ahead I saw the culprit fleeing from what looked like three squad cars behind him. With everyone's eyes locked on the criminal, no one seemed to see me soaring above the scene.

I swooped down about a block ahead of the Escalade, and waited for its arrival. As fast as it was coming, it didn't take very long.

I braced myself to prepare for the impact that was imminent. The driver, who had been paying more attention to the cops behind him than the road before him, looked up just in time to slam on the brakes before crashing into me. He jumped out of the SUV screaming at me while pointing his pistol at the officers who were now out of their cars and using their doors for shields. As the gunman yelled at me some more, I walked closer to him. When I got within ten feet from him he turned his gun away from the police and concentrated the barrel on me. After a few threats, and me ignoring those threats, he fired two shots into my chest. The bullets had no effect on my new diamond hard skin. I yanked the gun from his hands and slid it across the pavement to the cops. The criminal took a swing at me, but it was in vain. I picked him up and carried him to a spot in between his car and the police cars and then slammed him to the ground. The cops came running out from behind their cars and apprehended the man.

A few of the officers came over to see if I was ok. I assured them that the gunman's bullets missed me and that I was fine. They turned their attention back to the gunman and I sped off.

I felt exhilarated after that adrenaline rush. I got back to the motel as soon as I could, so I could try to find another adventure in the scanner.

It didn't take very long to find what I was looking for. There was a fire downtown, and an older lady was trapped on the top floor. With my super speed I was there in a matter of seconds.

The fire department hadn't made it there yet. I could hear their sirens, but there wasn't enough time to wait on them. I started jogging to the front door of the building, but right before getting to the door I was stopped by an officer.

"What are you doing?"

"I'm going in there to save her."

"You can't go in there. The fire blocks every possible way up."

"Just make sure the fire department has a ladder ready next to the window, so I can carry her down."

He continued to yell at me to not go in there as I walked away and entered the burning building.

The inside of the building was in full blaze. I walked straight thru all the flames, and up the stairs, until I reached the top floor. My skin may have been fire proof, but my clothes were not. When the old lady seen me and seen that I was on fire, she passed out on the floor. I wished for the fire on my clothes to go out, and then I picked up the old lady. The fire department was here now but they didn't have the ladder up yet. I could have easily flown the old lady down, but I didn't want to draw that attention on myself. Then I heard someone shout up, "The ladder isn't long enough to reach that high! You need to save yourself!"

I grabbed the old lady and ran to the other side of the building. I thought if everyone was gathered around on this side, maybe I could get her down on the other side without anyone seeing.

I was right. There was no one on the other side of the building. I leapt out the window and floated down to the pavement with the old lady thrown over my shoulder. I wished for the fire on the bottom floor to die down for a minute and then I walked in the back door and back out the front door.

When I walked out the front door, the outside crowd erupted with cheers. A couple firemen rushed over and grabbed the old lady and hustled her over to an ambulance. They came back to check me out, but of course I was fine. I needed to get away before the media got there. I dealt with them enough the first time they thought I was a hero. I didn't want to go through that again. They wouldn't think I was a hero anyways, if they knew only a few days before I set a building on fire and didn't help anyone.

After sneaking away, I started to go downtown and grab a bite to eat. I barely got a moment of peace before I heard a young lady scream, "Help! He's got my purse!"

I seen a man running with a purse clutched in his arms. I took off in pursuit of him. I easily caught up with him in no time. I grabbed the back of his shirt, stopping him in mid sprint. I turned his body so that he was facing me, then I yanked the purse out of his hands and slugged him in the face.

"You don't steal women's purses, asshole. Let's see you try to take my wallet."

He just continued to lay there on the ground.

A voice came from behind me, "Thank you so much." The voice sounded eerily familiar.

I turned around to give her back her purse.

"Brittany?"

Chapter 13
Explosive

My heart stopped for a second when I seen her face.

"Jaycin, is that you?"

"Yea. It's me. Here's your purse."

"What the hell happened to you? You look like shit."

"I was in a fire a few minutes ago." I really didn't feel like talking to her right now.

"Are you ok?"

"I'm fine."

"Where have you been? Why haven't you come home? I've tried calling your cell phone a million times."

I couldn't hold it in any longer. "Because I saw you in our old apartment with another guy. That's why I haven't came home, and why I won't ever be coming home again." She had a stunned look on her face as I walked away, leaving her standing there, alone. She knew I had seen her at the apartment, but I think it came as a surprise to her to know I knew she was in there with someone.

I went back to my desolate motel room to try to get her out of my head. It was a futile attempt as her face was now etched into my brain. The hurt that I was starting to get over was now back to square one. Just as I was near blowing my brains out, so that I could forget about her, there was a knock on the door.

When I opened the door no one was there. I looked around, but all I found was a news paper lying at my feet. The headline took me by surprise.

"Bomb in Neyland Stadium kills 25,000 people"

"That's impossible!" I thought to myself. I've been in Knoxville all week. I would have heard about something like that. As I observed the paper a little more closely, I found the reason for my ignorance. The paper was dated with tomorrow's date. If this paper was correct there would be an explosion that would go off tonight during the Tennessee versus Florida game. I checked my watch; it was 7:40 p.m. The game was set to start in five minutes.

I leapt off the balcony, and without crashing into a car this time, I took off through the sky. Once I made it to the stadium I had no idea where to start looking, and no time to spare. I wished that I knew where the bomb was.

I looked around for the clue that I knew I should be getting. I was looking for a giant X or a lit up section, but I didn't see anything. I glanced up at the score board to see how much more time I had before the game started. The game clock said it was one minute and twenty-six seconds before kick off; the more important thing on the score board was the letters on the jumbo-tron. "YY" That had to be my clue. The bomb was in section YY.

Now I was in section YY, but I still had no idea where the bomb was. I wished to be led to the bomb. Everything went silent except a faint ticking noise coming from somewhere close by. It wasn't coming from anyone in the stands. The noise was coming from under the seats. I followed the sound and it led me to a concession stand.

In the cooler, under twelve boxes of uncooked hotdogs, lay the ticking briefcase of destruction. I flipped open the case.

The concession workers, that I was previously unaware of, seen what I had possession of and started screaming and running in terror. If they seen what I seen when I opened the briefcase, then I can't blame them for their concern. The timer said the bomb was set to go off in thirty-two seconds.

I didn't have much time left to act; I had to get this bomb out of the stadium. I took off running up the steps until I made it to the top of the stadium. Time was of the essence and I had to make a choice. There were a lot of lives at jeopardy here, so if I didn't make the right choice, their blood would be on my hands. I hurled my body off the top of the stadium and shot myself, along with the briefcase, into the Tennessee River.

I swam the case down as far as I could until time wouldn't let me go any further. The case exploded in my arms. I couldn't see or feel anything except for a sharp pain in my head. The same pain I felt the day I hit my head on the pavement after pushing young Daniel Taylor out of the way of the SUV. And then, just like that day, everything went black.

Chapter 14
Awake

I was actually surprised when I opened my eyes. I didn't think there would be any way that I would survive something like a bomb explosion. However, it did do some damage, because when I woke up I was lying in a hospital bed with so many cords plugged into me I looked like a surge protector. My trying to grasp what kind of situation I was in was interrupted by a voice coming from the corner of the room.

"Welcome back. It's good to see you again."

It was the guardian angel child again. He climbed up in my bed and sat next to me.

"How did I survive that explosion?"

"Easy. There was no explosion."

"There was an explosion. I took the bomb from the football stadium, jumped in the river, and it exploded! It's the whole reason I'm in this hospital bed right now."

"There was NO explosion. You're in this hospital bed right now, because you were hit by an SUV when you saved Daniel Taylor."

"Saved Daniel Taylor!? That was two years ago!" I was kind of frustrated, but he looked calm. He spoke very gently as he brushed my hair out of my face.

"No, that was weeks ago. Three weeks to be exact. You've been unconscious since then. I'm glad you're finally awake though. That means it's almost time for your reward."

I was shocked by the words that were coming out his tiny mouth. There was no way he could be telling the truth. Everything that happened since that day had seemed so real.

"So, what is my reward then?"

"You'll find out soon enough."

"Well, whatever it is, I'm going to use it for good. No more selfishness from me. From now on, as soon as I get out of this bed, I'm going to live my life the right way." If I had learned anything from whatever it was that went on during my comatose state, it was selfishness leads to sadness.

"I'm sorry."

He was looking off to the side now, like he was trying to avoid looking at me. "Sorry for what?" His sad face worried me.

"You don't get to leave the bed. The only reason you're awake now, is because God wants to let you say your goodbyes."

"Goodbyes? What are you saying?"

"You're not going to make it, Jaycin. Make the most of what little time you have left."

Tears started to build in the corners of my eyes. "But I feel fine. Why wouldn't I make it?"

"It's your time. You've done your duty here on earth."

"But…But I thought my reward is coming soon?" I couldn't fight the tears back any longer.

"It is. You will be rewarded greatly. Trust me on that."

He got up and climbed out of my bed.

"Where are you going?"

"I have to leave now. You have some visitors coming."

He was walking towards the door, but just vanished into thin air on his way out.

Before I had time to let everything he said sink in, my parents walked into the room. When I saw them, I knew everything he said was true and I was glad of it. I may be dying now, but they're still alive. It was a fair trade-off in my eyes. I wiped the tears from my face.

"Jaycin! You're awake!" My tears were gone now but my mother's were just beginning.

"Hey son. You feeling ok?" My dad was never one to get all excited, but I could hear it in his voice that he was glad I was awake.

"Yea, I'm fine. Look mom and dad, I know I've never been the best son in the world, or a son you could brag about, or be proud of..." I was cut off by my mom.

"Don't talk like that, Jaycin. We are very proud of you. We seen the video of what you did, and it was horrifying, but to know we raised a son who would risk his life like that, for a total stranger...Well, I can't think of anything you could do to make us more proud of you than we are right now." The tears were pouring out of her eyes now.

"We're both very proud of you, son. We always have been." It was the first time my dad had ever said anything like that to me before.

"While I have you both here, I need to tell you something. I love you guys. I'm sorry for everything I've ever put you through. I just wanted you both to know that. I love you both and I'm sorry I haven't said it very often."

"We love you, too. And we promise we'll say it more often." My mom was still balling like a baby.

Tthanks, but I doubt you'll have many more chances."

"What are you talking about? You're awake now. You're getting better." It sounded like my dad was trying to convince himself, rather than me.

"Yea, maybe." I decided not to tell them I was about to die. I didn't want to see them hurting more than they already were. They probably wouldn't have believed me anyway.

My mom came closer and wrapped her arms around me. "We're going to go out now and let you get some rest. You have someone else who wants to see you, too."

"Goodnight, son."

"Bye, dad. Bye, mom. I love you."

"I love you too, baby."

"Yea, love you son."

Chapter 15
Final Words

Watching my parents walk out of the room tore me up on the inside. I knew, chances were, I would never see them again. I felt like just closing my eyes and letting my time come, but just then you walked in. I knew as soon as I seen you I had to tell you this story.

"Can I ask you something, Mr. Smith?"

"Sure, Daniel. Go right ahead."

"If you wouldn't have tried saving me you wouldn't be dying. So, do you hate me? Do you regret what you did?"

"I've always wanted to leave this world with a life I could be proud of, that anyone would be proud of. I wanted my life to have a meaning. Being forgotten was not an option that I would be satisfied with."

"Now, because of you, when people speak my name they will think "Hero." Parents will want their children to grow up to be as selfless as me. People will forget about the first twenty-eight years of my life. All their going to remember is how it ended."

"Dying for the greater good; who would have expected that out of me? I wouldn't have before today. I was a nobody. I've accomplished nothing. I've helped no one. It's never even crossed my mind."

"If I would have just ignored those instincts for those few seconds I would still be alive. All it would have taken was for me to look away. Turn my back and head in the other direction. But who would have remembered me? What would my life had meant when I finally left this world? Nothing."

"So if you're asking me if giving my life for this was worth it. Yes. Yes it was."

"But I don't want you to die Mr. Smith."

"It's ok Daniel. It's my time. I know you can't understand that right now, but trust me; I'm going to be fine. My reward is still coming."

"But it's all my fault that you're going to die."

"Please don't cry, Daniel. You did me a huge favor. My life has completely turned around, and I owe it all to you."

"Is there anything I can do to help you?"

"Yes. There is one thing. You can tell people my story. Share with people who need to hear it. Maybe it can help make a difference."

"Ok, Mr. Smith. I will, I promise."

"Ok. Well, I think I'm going to go to sleep now, Daniel. Thank you for stopping by. I'll be seeing you soon."

Epilogue
Daniel Taylor

Mr. Smith's heart stopped beating seconds after he closed his eyes for that final time. It's been thirty years since that day and still yet, not a day has gone by where I haven't thought about him or thanked God for giving us people like him on this earth.

Not only did that day he saved me change his life; it also changed my life forever.

My life was not going very well at that time. My parents were going through a divorce and school was getting really tough on me. I had been getting picked on at school every day for the past few months by a group of guys at my school. They would knock the books out of my hands whenever I would walk by; they would try to shove my head in a toilet every day before I went home. I was already going through a lot, but they made my life pure hell.

At that time I had never been brought up to believe in God. I didn't really know anything about him. If I did, then that day may have turned out different.

That morning I was running a little late for school. I started out the door on time, but I had those bullies on my mind. For a while I had been wanting to do something about it, I just never had the courage. That morning, as I was on my way to school, I decided it was time to go through with it. I ran back home and got my dad's loaded gun out from under his bed. I shoved it in my backpack and started back on my way to school.

When Mr. Smith pushed me out of the way of that SUV, I was actually walking down the road planning out how I was going to kill them. I was just listening to my iPod, off in a daze, imagining how it was all going to go down.

After Mr. Smith saved me, and was hit by the vehicle, I was scared. After the people looked at me to make sure I was ok, I ran behind a building and threw my backpack into a large dumpster. I spent the next three weeks going to the hospital every day hoping to see him wake up and get better. I felt terrible for being the cause of him being hurt. Especially since I knew what was going through my mind at that time.

When Mr. Smith finally did wake up and told me that story, it changed my life forever. It opened up a new world for me. If someone could risk his life for someone as insignificant as me, and not regret it because he knew it's what God wanted, then maybe this God is someone I should get to know.

I spent the rest of my high school and college years concentrating on my studies and using whatever free time I had to learn about God.

Since then I have spent the last twenty-years going around the country, and different parts of the world, telling them the story of Jaycin Smith and trying to teach people about God.